Acer
pseudoplatanus

CUENTO
DE LUZ

For Andrea, il mio grande amore,
who sows so many good things in me.

- Carla Balzaretti -

To all of the wonderful people in my life, who sow
their seeds so that our world can be a little bit better.

- Sonja Wimmer -

The Gardener's Surprise

Text © Carla Balzaretti
Illustrations © Sonja Wimmer
This edition © 2013 Cuento de Luz SL
Calle Claveles 10 | Urb Monteclaro | Pozuelo de Alarcón | 28223 | Madrid | Spain
www.cuentodeluz.com
Title in Spanish: La sorpresa del jardinero
English translation by Jon Brokenbrow

ISBN: 978-84-15784-60-9

Printed by Shanghai Chenxi Printing Co., Ltd. January 2014, print number 1407-2

The Gardener's Surprise

Carla Balzaretti & Sonja Wimmer

A long time ago, in a city far, far away, lived Andrew, a mechanic who repaired old freight trains.

Andrew wasn't just a mechanic. He was also an amateur gardener. He was one of those people who truly loved plants, who knew their names and species by heart, and spent his time marveling at the colors and shapes of the flowers.

He was an amateur gardener because he lived in a small apartment on the fourth floor, without a balcony or a terrace. And so it was quite difficult for him to make furrows in the earth, plant the seeds and water them until the first shoots appeared.

Even so, every day he would spend a few hours taking care of the flowers that grew in pots carefully arranged in his small living room. Well, not just in his living room.

And he would dream. He would often dream about great expanses of fertile land. Black, moist land gazing up towards the sky, waiting for a shower of seeds.

His plants had also taken over the garden, the bathroom, the hallway, the bedrooms, and even grew in open drawers.

Some nights, Andrew and his family had eaten dinner in the company of a group of yellow tulips.

His wife and his children also dreamt about great swathes of fertile land. It was quite tricky having to brush your teeth with a Chinese rose bush in the washbasin.

Andrew's bosses would say that Andrew was the type of mechanic who could bring any type of train destined for the junkyard back to life.

He worked hard on the trains, but he didn't earn much money. While he repaired the broken parts, he would imagine the trains chugging down the track full of lilies. Or he would think of funny meanings for their scientific names.

"*Calendula officinalis*, or the office marigold," he would chuckle to himself, imagining a radiant marigold sitting behind a desk.

DIANTHUS BARBATUS   DIANTHUS PLUMARIUS

Surrounded by wrenches and motors, Andrew would go over his seed collection in his mind and ask himself: "What would a *Dianthus barbatus* look like? A charming barber called

Sweet William, with a long moustache? And a *Dianthus plumarius*? A flower with brightly-colored feathers? Could the *Strelitzia* or bird of paradise really fly?

One day, his boss told him that an important company was looking for the best mechanics in the area. Andrew was one of them.

Apart from a good salary, they offered him a house with a big garden. He accepted immediately.

While he picked up his belongings in the old station, he imagined himself watering the beautiful exotic plants that would grow on his land.

It didn't take long for Andrew to get his first surprise. He would no longer be spending his time on old trains and broken down locomotives. Now he would be working on airplanes. He felt a little nervous about his new job, but he said to himself, "Really, they're just a bunch

of screws, metal and patience. It doesn't matter what shape they are." And Andrew began to imagine the hangar filling with lilies, orchids and marigolds. Office marigolds, barbers named Sweet William, pink-feathered flowers, and birds with petals for feathers.

His second surprise was even bigger. He wasn't just going to be working on planes, but on war planes! Andrew was hired to load bombs into the planes that were flying off to war. A war that had been declared between several far-off

countries. Countries whose names he could hardly pronounce. His hands would be used to get the planes ready to drop bombs on fields and forests, but also on cities, buildings, schools, people, on all living things.

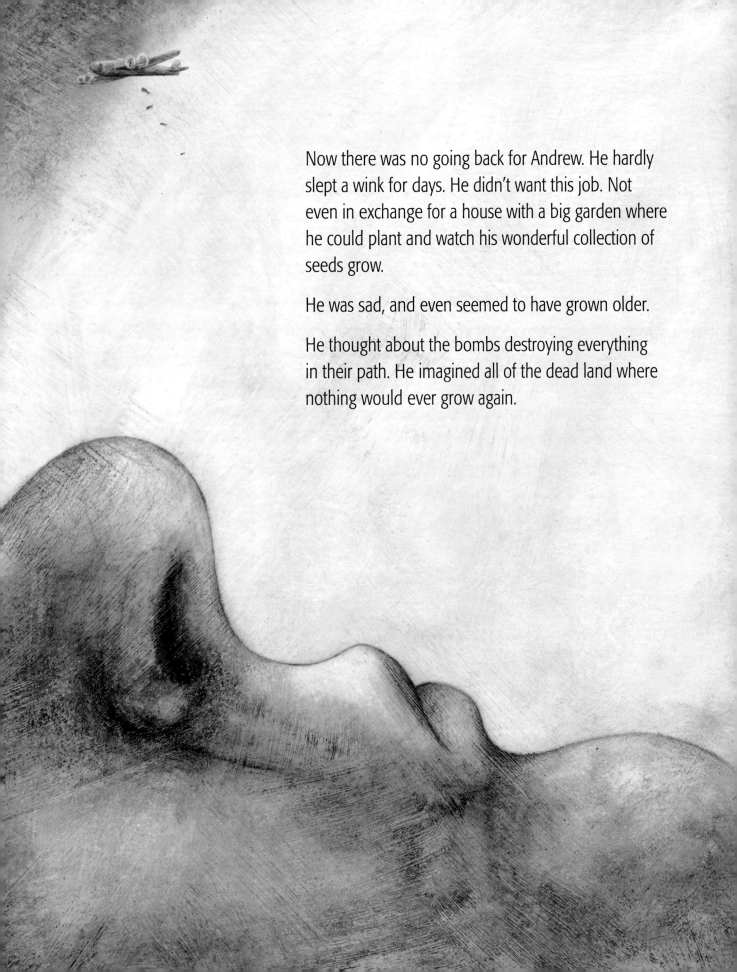

Now there was no going back for Andrew. He hardly slept a wink for days. He didn't want this job. Not even in exchange for a house with a big garden where he could plant and watch his wonderful collection of seeds grow.

He was sad, and even seemed to have grown older.

He thought about the bombs destroying everything in their path. He imagined all of the dead land where nothing would ever grow again.

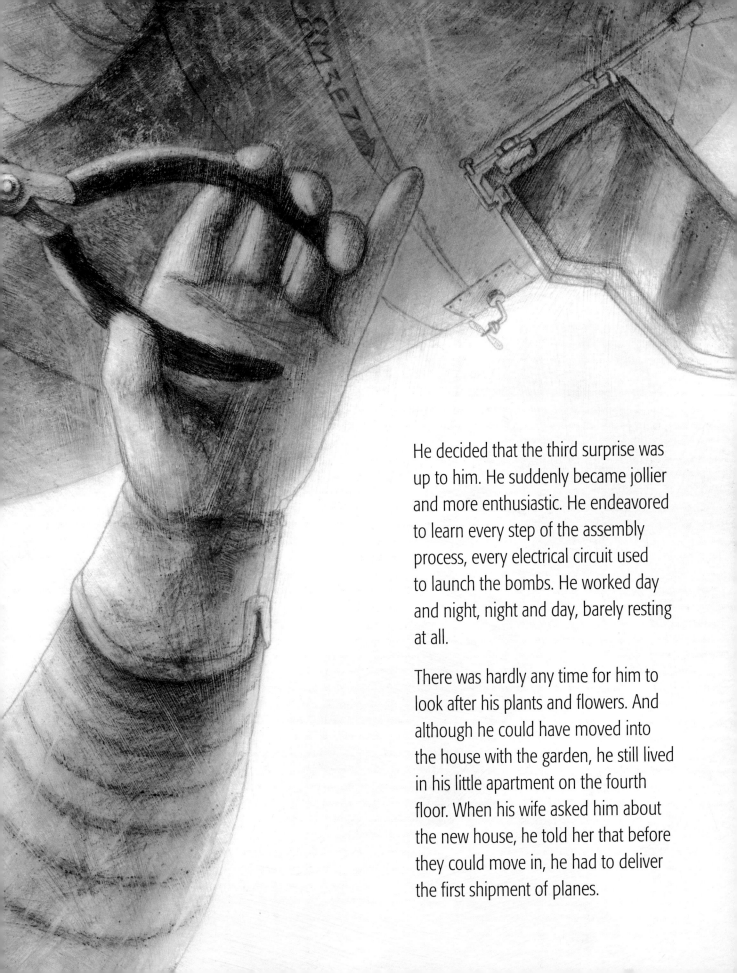

He decided that the third surprise was up to him. He suddenly became jollier and more enthusiastic. He endeavored to learn every step of the assembly process, every electrical circuit used to launch the bombs. He worked day and night, night and day, barely resting at all.

There was hardly any time for him to look after his plants and flowers. And although he could have moved into the house with the garden, he still lived in his little apartment on the fourth floor. When his wife asked him about the new house, he told her that before they could move in, he had to deliver the first shipment of planes.

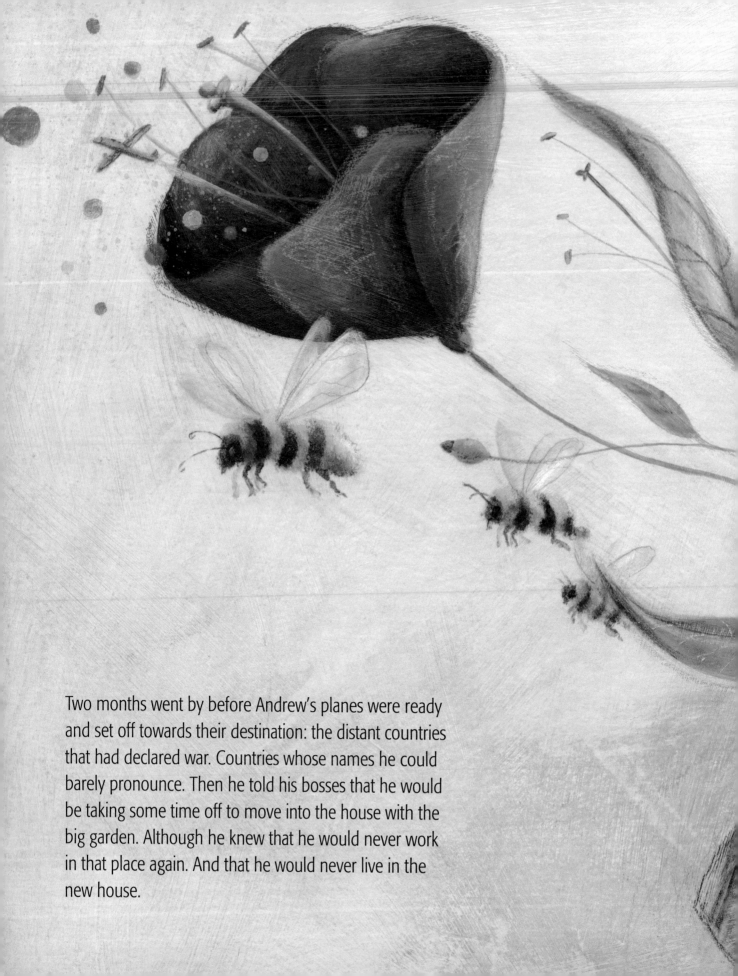

Two months went by before Andrew's planes were ready and set off towards their destination: the distant countries that had declared war. Countries whose names he could barely pronounce. Then he told his bosses that he would be taking some time off to move into the house with the big garden. Although he knew that he would never work in that place again. And that he would never live in the new house.

Inside the planes, instead of bombs, he had put every imaginable type of flower seeds: his seed collection, the ones he was keeping to plant in the house of his dreams.

Andrew had found an even larger garden. A wide expanse of fertile soil. Black, moist soil gazing up towards the sky, waiting for a shower of seeds.

And he thought that it would be better to sow them with tulips, lilies, marigolds and carnations—office marigolds, barbers named Sweet William, pink-feathered flowers, and birds with petals for feathers, flying off to paradise.